P9-AOT-085

SEP 2021

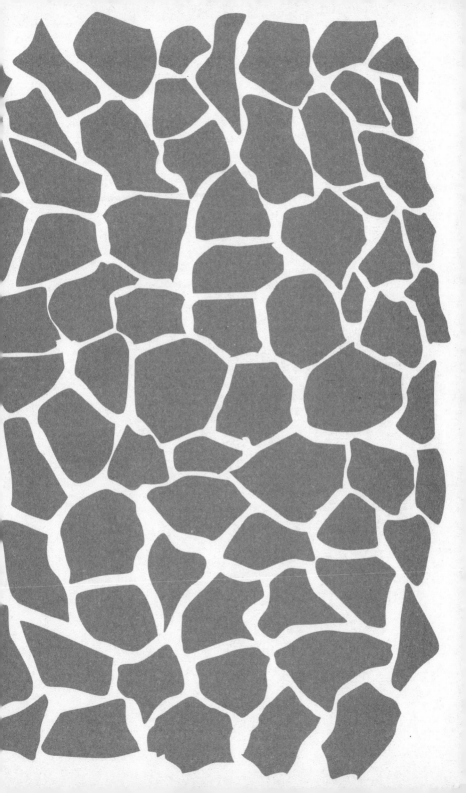

MYSTERIES ON ZOO LANE #3

Zebra at the Zoo

#3
MYSTERIES ON ZOO LANE

Zebra at the Zoo

Patricia Reilly Giff

illustrated by
Abby Carter

HOLIDAY HOUSE · NEW YORK

Text copyright © 2021 by Patricia Reilly Giff

Art copyright © 2021 by Abby Carter

All Rights Reserved

HOLIDAY HOUSE is registered in the U.S. Patent and Trademark Office.

Printed and bound in January 2021 at Maple Press, York, PA, USA.

www.holidayhouse.com

First Edition

1 3 5 7 9 10 8 6 4 2

Library of Congress Cataloging-in-Publication Data

Names: Giff, Patricia Reilly, author. | Carter, Abby, illustrator.

Title: Zebra at the zoo / by Patricia Reilly Giff;
illustrated by Abby Carter.

Description: First edition. | New York : Holiday House, 2021.

Series: Mysteries on Zoo Lane ; book 3 | Audience: Ages 7–10.

Audience: Grades 2–3. | Summary: Alex sneaks into the zoo to visit his favorite
animal, but when a cat sneaks through the same hole and gets lost he must find
her before any of the other animals do.

Identifiers: LCCN 2020020617 | ISBN 9780823446681 (hardcover)

ISBN 9780823449071 (paperback)

Subjects: CYAC: Lost and found possessions—Fiction. | Zoos—Fiction.

Zoo animals—Fiction. | Mystery and detective stories.

Classification: LCC PZ7.G3626 Ze 2021 | DDC [Fic]—dc23

LC record available at https://lccn.loc.gov/2020020617

ISBN: 978-0-8234-4668-1 (hardcover)

ISBN: 978-0-8234-4907-1 (paperback)

ISBN: 978-0-8234-4905-7 (ebook)

Love to my boys

MYSTERIES ON ZOO LANE

#3

Zebra
at the
Zoo

CHAPTER 1

SCHOOL again!

Mom had bought Alex a new shirt. It was scratchy with lines going up and down.

Worse, he was going to have that strict teacher, Mrs. Silver.

"Hurry, Alex," Mom called. "You don't want to be late."

Alex really was in a hurry. First, he wanted to stop at the zoo.

"See you later, Mom," he yelled.

She called something back. Was it about Oreo, his cat?

He didn't have time to wait. Not if he wanted to see the red panda.

Not many were left in the world. Zoos were trying to save them.

He'd stopped to see the panda every day this summer.

He rushed down Zoo Lane and turned the corner.

He slid to a stop.

The huge iron gates were shut.

The zoo wasn't open yet.

Never mind. He knew how to get in.

He threaded his way along the outside.

There were a million weeds.

Maybe even poison ivy.

Too bad. He knew there was a hole in the fence. It was large enough to crawl through.

He could do it.

He stopped on one foot. Was that the schoolyard bell? Were the kids lining up already?

But there was the opening.

He sank down and crawled through.

He felt his shirt rip. Mom wouldn't be happy.

He went around the bushes and stood up.

The panda's forest area was along the path.

Bamboo thickets grew there. Red pandas loved bamboo.

He crossed his fingers. If only she wouldn't be hiding.

"Hey," a voice yelled.

Alex ducked.

It was a keeper. He wore a baseball hat over his eyes.

Alex had never seen him before.

The iron gates slid across. The zoo was open.

He looked up. The keeper's hands were on his hips.

Alex shook his head. If only he'd waited outside for a minute.

"What are you doing here?" the keeper asked.

He sounded angry. Worse than angry.

"It's the first day of school. It was my only chance to see the red panda." He stopped to take a breath. "She's the best."

"Enough!" the keeper said. "I'm taking you to the office."

"I'll be late for school," Alex said. "I'll be in trouble."

"You're in trouble now," the keeper told him.

Alex looked at the gate. It was only steps away.

He took a chance.

He ran.

CHAPTER 2

ALEX was a mess.

His shirt sleeve was flapping.
His jeans were dirty.

He was the last one in the
classroom.

"Sit anywhere." The teacher
waved her hands around.

Alex couldn't believe it. It

wasn't the strict teacher. This one was new.

Her hair hung down over her eyes.

Alex dived into a seat next to the window.

He could see the zoo from here. Some of it, anyway.

He'd watch the leopards, panda, bobcats, and even the pack of wild wolves.

Starting this summer, he had read about zoo animals.

He'd learned about the red panda. She had lived in China and the Himalayan Mountains.

It was cold there. Freezing.

The panda had fur on the soles of her feet. It kept her warm.

He was glad he could watch her from the window.

He'd never be able to go to the zoo again. Not even to see Dad.

Dad worked there every day. He made sure the animals had the food they needed.

The zoo was Dad's favorite place. And Alex's too.

Alex felt his eyes burning.

But something else. Suppose the keeper came to school looking for him?

What would happen?

He tried not to think of it.

He hunched up to look outside the window.

Leopard babies were sleeping near the fence. Last year they were only fifteen pounds. Now they were about a hundred. Not really babies anymore.

The new teacher clapped her hands.

He took a last look outside.

He saw a bobcat with its short tail. It was stalking something in the trees. Maybe a rabbit.

Poor rabbit.

The bobcat reminded Alex of his cat, Oreo. But Oreo had a long skinny tail. She had lots of black-and-white stripes.

Alex turned to look at the teacher.

He heard a wolf howling.

Alex made a quiet wolf growl to himself.

He was good at animal sounds.

The girl next to him raised her

hand. "Can I change my seat? Alex is growling at me."

"No, at myself," he said. "I was thinking of wolves."

Maybe the teacher wasn't listening. She was writing on the chalkboard: Zoo Animals.

The girl made wolf claws at him with her fingers.

What was her name?

Callie. Right. The one with the ponytail. It was always swinging back and forth.

The teacher dusted off her hands. "I love projects," she said.

Alex just had to tell her! "We

made maps of the school last year," he said.

Could anything be worse than that?

"Alex never raises his hand," Callie said.

"You'll love this project," the teacher told the class.

She wrote her name on the chalkboard: Mrs. Hall.

Alex looked out the window.

The bobcat was climbing a thin tree.

If only Alex were at the zoo.

He'd lean against the fence.

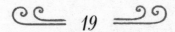

He'd look at the bobcat up close.

Most of all he'd say hello to the red panda.

"We'll do a project with the zoo," the teacher said. "We'll write about an animal."

Alex sat up. What was she saying?

What could he do?

He couldn't go to the zoo.

Not this year.

Maybe never again.

CHAPTER 3

MRS. Hall smiled at them. "We'll go around the room now. We'll each choose an animal."

She pointed to the first row.

Mitchell said, "Bear."

"Anteater," Tori said.

They went back and forth. "Prairie dog, otter, alligator."

Alex knew what he'd pick, of course. The red panda.

She was his favorite. And he wouldn't have to go to the zoo. He knew all about her.

"Leopard," Ellen said.

Suppose someone picked the red panda?

Lots of kids were before him. He couldn't wait any longer.

He yelled it out. "Red panda!
They're almost extinct. That means
there aren't many left in the world."

"Not fair," Callie said. Her face
was all scrunched up. "Alex is out
of turn. And I wanted the panda."

"They're not big," Alex cut in. "But they're fierce."

The teacher tilted her head. "You're excited about this project, Alex. I see that."

She knew his name already. That was a surprise.

"We'll give Callie the panda," Mrs. Hall said. "How about a wolf for you, Alex? You made a great wolf growl."

Wolves were the worst. They hunted small animals in a pack. Nothing could escape them.

Mrs. Hall was looking at someone else.

Alex gave it one more try. "I read about red pandas." But Luke was talking. "Maybe a meerkat?"

"Neat idea," Mrs. Hall said. "That will be fun."

Alex put his head down on his desk.

It was a long way to the weekend.

It was even a long way to the end of this day.

It was forever until summertime again.

CHAPTER 4

SCHOOL was over for the day.
Alex turned into Zoo Lane.

Nana-Next-Door was outside.
She was digging in her garden.

Her dog, Hero, shook himself.
Mud sprayed all over the place.

Never mind. He was a great
dog.

Nana looked up. She grinned. "Too hot for school. Right?"

"I guess so."

"Hey." She walked down the path. "You don't look happy."

Hero walked with her. He left paw prints on the path.

Alex bent down and hugged the dog.

Out back, a lion roared.

Or maybe it was a leopard. Did leopards roar?

"What's wrong?" Nana asked. "Is it something with school?"

He raised his shoulders. "It's everything."

He didn't mean to say anything else.

But he couldn't stop.

He told her about Callie and the red panda. "And now I'm stuck with the wolf," he said.

Nana tilted her head.

"Even worse," he said. "I can never go back to the zoo."

"Never is a long time," Nana said.

Was he going to cry? "This morning I snuck in early. A keeper saw me, so I ran."

Nana said, "Let's see about all this."

She put her hands on his arms. "We'll talk to the keeper."

He tried to swallow. And was that his heart hammering?

"I might have run away too," Nana said. "But we have to go back."

She threw her trowel in the weeds.

Hero headed for the patio. He liked to nap in the shade.

Alex couldn't run away from Nana.

But suppose the keeper was still angry?

What then?

Alex followed her along Zoo Lane.

But he went slowly.

If only he could change her mind.

CHAPTER 5

THE zoo was noisy this afternoon.

Birds chittered. A raven cawed.

Alex heard a wolf howl. It almost made him shiver.

"You haven't met Clem yet," Nana said.

He shook his head.

"He's a new keeper. He loves

to take care of wild animals. He says they're important."

"Does he wear a baseball hat?"

"Sure," Nana said. "It must be as old as he is."

Clem must be that keeper!

They went through the iron gates and along the path.

"Keep looking," Nana said. "We'll go toward the back."

Alex saw Callie running out of the zoo. Her ponytail was swinging.

Up ahead was Wolves' World. Inside, there were some trees, and bushes . . .

Wolf World

And a pack of wolves, of course.

They didn't look friendly.

But the keeper did. He grinned at them. He was wearing a blue baseball cap.

It looked about a hundred years old.

The keeper looked a hundred years old too.

"That's Clem," Nana said.

Alex shook his head at Nana. Clem wasn't the one.

Nana-Next-Door smiled back at Clem.

"This is Alex," she said. "He likes animals. He likes to talk too. But he's had a little trouble today."

Clem pushed back his cap. He had almost no hair.

He nodded at Alex. "I like kids who talk."

He pointed to a bench. "Let's sit for a minute."

Alex sat at one end. It was hot. It still felt like summer.

If only . . .

There were too many "if onlys" to count.

Then Alex saw another keeper. He had a baseball hat too.

Alex was ready to run again.

The keeper saw Alex too. He stopped.

"I'm sorry," Alex whispered.

The keeper nodded. "All right, I guess. I'm worried about something else."

Alex took a breath.

"A cat is in here somewhere,"

the keeper said. "I hope she's all right. I tried to catch her. She was just too fast for me."

"All these wild animals," Clem said. "It's dangerous for a cat."

Lucky that Oreo was home.

She liked to sit under the kitchen table. She always waited for food.

"I don't know how it got in,"the keeper said.

The hole in the fence! Alex almost said it aloud. But the zoo people would fix it then.

And suppose the cat waited until the gates were closed?

How could she get out again?

Alex watched the keeper walk down the path again.

He wasn't in trouble anymore. He could come back to the zoo every day.

He was worried about that

poor cat, though. What if she went into Wolves' World?

Nana-Next-Door was smiling. "All right now, Alex," she said. She gave his arm a pat.

"This week we're having a zoo project," Clem said. "I talked to Mrs. Hall. She had everyone pick an animal. So we're almost ready to begin."

Mrs. Hall. His teacher.

Clem was talking about their class.

"I want to see kids who write about wild animals," Clem said. "And why we should save them."

Alex looked over his shoulder.

The wolves were lying in the shade, half asleep.

One of them was panting. Alex could see its long tongue and its curved teeth.

If only he could write about the red panda.

But what could he say about a pack of wolves?

Weren't they cruel?

Wasn't everyone always afraid of them?

And why not!

Right now, one of them opened its mouth wide.

It howled.

Even Clem jumped. "That's the way they talk to each other," he said.

Alex saw a baby wolf. It was tumbling over its mother.

Clem nodded at him. "Something good in everything," he said.

"I guess," Alex said.

He wasn't sure he believed it, though.

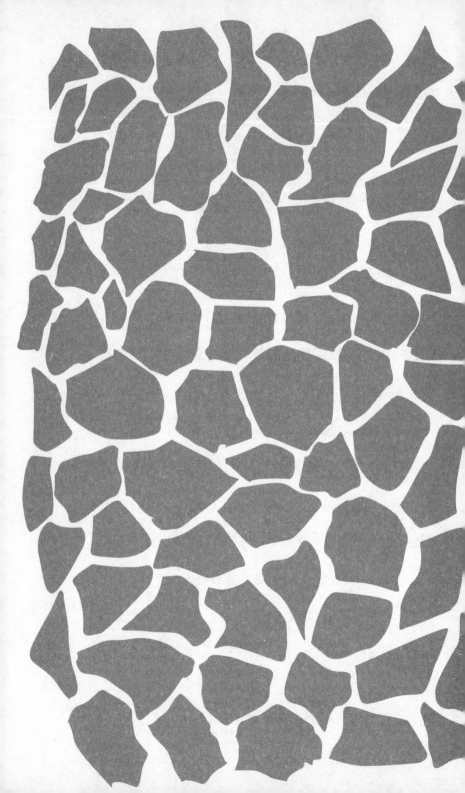

CHAPTER 6

Mom met him at the door.

"Where have you been? Did you have a good day? I've been worried."

Mom liked to talk a lot too, Alex thought. "Don't worry. I'm all right."

"I'm really upset about Oreo," she told him.

"Is she sick? Isn't she under the table?"

Mom shook her head. "I've looked through the house. She hardly ever gets outside. But I can't find her."

Mom raised her shoulders. "She isn't anywhere."

Alex felt his heart thumping again.

The cat in the zoo!

Was it his cat?

"I'll look for her outside," he said.

Mom nodded.

Alex ran back to the zoo.

It was still open.

He ran up one path. Then he skittered down the next.

He kept calling. But he didn't see her.

At last he went back home.

Alex and Mom waited through dinner.

Dad was still at the zoo. If only he'd find Oreo. He'd bring her home right away.

Now Alex knew what Mom must have called to him this morning.

Make sure you close the door.

He hadn't.

It was his fault that Oreo was
gone.

CHAPTER 7

THE next day was trip day. Alex almost forgot his permission slip.

He had to go back home for it.

He left the kitchen door open a little bit. Maybe Oreo would come home.

"Let's go," the teacher said after the pledge.

Everyone raced to the side of the room.

They weren't going far. Just down Zoo Lane and into the zoo.

"We're about to meet a man named Clem," Mrs. Hall said. "He knows all about animals. 'The wilder the better,' he says."

Alex nodded to himself.

On the way, he kept an eye out for Oreo.

Alex was tired. He'd stayed awake last night. He kept waiting to hear her meow at the door.

Dad had come in. He hadn't seen her either.

Now Clem waited for them in a large room. The walls were covered with pictures: llamas, bears, bobcats, and even a chicken.

Or maybe it was a rooster.

"Grab a seat," Clem said.

Alex sat next to Luke, the new boy.

Lucky Luke. His father was the zoo doctor. He could see the baby animals whenever he wanted.

Clem went to the chalkboard. He drew a bunch of circles in a line.

He was a terrible artist.

The circles were lopsided. So were the lines that joined them.

Alex tilted his head. Was Clem drawing a necklace like Mom's? A chain anyway.

He must have said it aloud.

"Yes," Clem said. "A food

chain. These lines link them together."

Luke raised his hand. "My dad said if one group of animals is extinct, everything goes wrong."

"Yes!" Clem pointed to the first circle. "These might be grasses."

"I've got it," Luke said. "A rabbit eats the grass."

Clem smiled. "And then a hawk is hungry. It needs food."

Mitchell nodded. "The hawk pounces on the rabbit."

"One thing depends on

another," Clem said. "All the way up. . . ."

He drew an X over the first circle. "Suppose there was no grass? What would happen to the rabbit? And then to the hawk?"

Mrs. Hall was nodding.

"Think of that as you write," Clem said. "Learn what's happening in your animal's world. How is it part of the food chain?"

He grinned at them. "And now, there's lunch in your world! I hope it's good."

Outside, the class stopped at the park area to eat.

Alex watched a llama behind them. Its cheeks were moving. It looked like a cow chewing its cud.

A llama would have been better than writing about a wolf.

Much better.

He'd talk to Mrs. Hall. Maybe she'd let him pick a different animal.

He tried to think. No one had picked the llama.

And what about a bear?

He thought about polar bears, who lived in the ice and snow.

He had to talk Mrs. Hall into a great animal. He just had to.

CHAPTER 8

THE next day was Saturday.

School would wait until Monday. He'd talk to Mrs. Hall then.

Today he'd go back to the zoo. He'd search for Oreo. She had to be somewhere.

He had to find her.

If only she hadn't sneaked into

Wolves' World or Lions' Lair.
If only she was all right.

Would she be hungry? Or maybe thirsty?

He'd race home with her. He'd fill her bowl with cool water. He'd give her a plate of kibbles.

She'd have everything she needed.

Later, he'd come back to see the wolves. Maybe Mrs. Hall wouldn't change her mind.

"I'll be back soon, Mom," he called.

He passed Nana-Next-Door on his way.

"Off to the zoo?" she asked. "Lucky guy."

He nodded. Usually he'd stop to talk to her. But there was no time today.

He darted around the corner. He rushed through the open gates.

"Oreo," he called. "Please come home."

But then he saw Callie. She was sitting on a bench. It was near the red panda's forest. He walked past her.

Was she crying?

He looked back. Yes. Her face was red.

She reached up. She wiped her eyes on the edge of her shirt.

What was the matter? Why was she crying?

She saw him. She turned away quickly.

He took another step. Then he stopped. He sank on the bench near her.

What could he say?

He saw the red panda. She was sharpening her claws on a tree.

He heard Callie sniffle.

"What's the matter?" he said at last.

"Nothing," she said. "Why are you sitting here?"

He said it before he thought. "Maybe I could help."

She didn't say anything.

The panda was chewing something now. He'd read that they ate roots and acorns. They liked fruit.

Sometimes they ate young birds and birds' eggs. They were part of the food chain.

He waited awhile. "What's the matter?" he asked again.

She spread her hands. "Just everything."

"Me too," he said. "Everything."

"I don't know one thing about wild animals," Callie said.

"Then why did you pick the red panda?"

He tried not to sound angry.

"I have a panda at home," she said.

"Really?"

"Not a real one. But I sleep with it at night. I'm afraid of the dark."

Sometimes he was afraid of the dark too. He never told anyone that.

"And my mom has allergies," she said.

What did that have to do with pandas?

"She won't let me keep my cat, Zebra."

"That's an odd name for a cat," he said.

Callie didn't answer for a moment. She wiped her eyes. "How can I just let her go? She'll be so hungry and thirsty."

Everyone had a cat worry, Alex thought.

But Callie was right. How could you just let a cat go?

"I don't know what to do about anything," she said

"I guess I could tell you about the red panda," he said.

He leaned forward.

Why had he said that?

She turned to look at him. "I know you wanted the panda. I'm sorry."

He shook his head. "The red panda's name in Latin is *colored cat*."

What else? He tried to think. Yes. "They have a tail with rings. There's an almost real thumb on their wrists. It helps them climb."

He was out of breath.

Callie was staring at him.

"I'll try to think of more," he said.

"Even this is a lot," she said. "Thank you."

She took a breath too. "Would you like to have a cat?"

He shook his head. Did she see he was almost crying?

He couldn't say any more.

He just wanted his own cat.

And he thought his own cat wanted him.

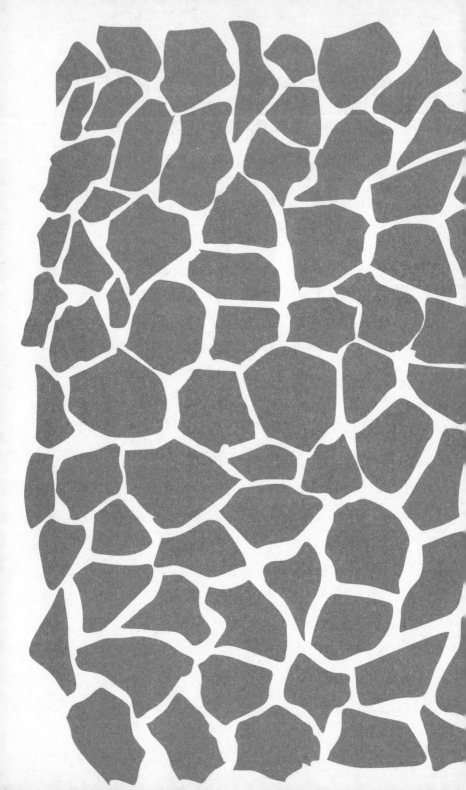

CHAPTER 9

IT was Monday again.

What could he say to Mrs. Hall? He'd write about almost any animal. If only it wasn't the wolf.

Mrs. Hall was standing in the schoolyard.

"Alex," she called when she saw him.

She began to talk before he did.

"I have something for you," she said. "A book I love."

She reached into her backpack. She pulled it out. "I thought of you all weekend."

He opened his mouth.

"It's about wolves." She handed it to him. "I've been waiting to give it to you."

"Thanks," he said. How could he ask her to change animals now? What would she think?

"People don't like wolves," she said. "But I know you do. You'll

love the gray wolf. And the red wolf is almost extinct."

He had to say something.

Say anything, he told himself.

"I'll read it as soon as I can. All of it."

"You'll be a terrific wolf boy," she said.

The bell rang. There wasn't time for more.

He headed for his line.

"Have fun with it," Mrs. Hall called. "Read and then write."

"I will," he said.

He had to!

He stood behind Callie.

"Good," she said. "I wanted to ask you. Do you cry a lot?"

What a thing to ask!

"I was wondering about it," she said.

"Everyone says that's baby-ish," he said after a minute.

He hoped no one was listening.

"You were crying at the zoo," she said.

"I had a good reason."

If he told her why, he really would cry.

But she was waiting. He had to say something.

"I lost my cat. She's somewhere in the zoo."

"Your cat?" Her hand went to her mouth.

She said it again. "Your cat."

"I don't know what happened to her."

The line was moving. But Callie stood still. "What does she look like?"

"She has a long skinny tail." He ran his fingers up and down in the air. "She has black-and-white stripes."

"Zebra!" Callie grabbed his arm.

"I know what happened. Let me tell you."

The rest of the line moved around them.

"A black-and-white cat was

wandering around," Callie said. "I picked her up . . ."

"You found my cat?" He was crying now.

"Yes." Callie twirled. "I'm so happy. The cat will be happy. My mom will be happy."

"I'll be happy," Alex said.

They began to walk with the line.

Oreo would be back home this afternoon. Zebra!

What could be better?

He didn't even mind writing about wolves.

Maybe he'd find out what

Clem had been telling them about food chains.

What a great school year this was turning out to be. And even Callie was a new friend.

WHAT ALEX WROTE

THE WOLF

Many Native Americans say that wolves teach us how important family is. They learn to hunt for food together. The Ojibwa consider wolves to be great teachers to humans.

A pack of wolves could be called a family. There's a mother, a father, and young wolves.

They take care of each other. They hunt together. And they help other animals. As soon as they kill, ravens fly down to eat. Coyotes wait until the wolves leave. Then they have a meal.

And wolves may leave fast. Bears chase them. They want to eat too.

Wolves are part of the food chain. But some wolf families are endangered. What would happen if they were gone? The chain would be missing a link. Zoos will see that this doesn't happen.

READ MORE OF THE

MYSTERIES ON ZOO LANE!

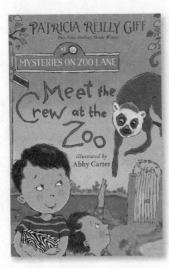

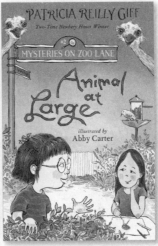

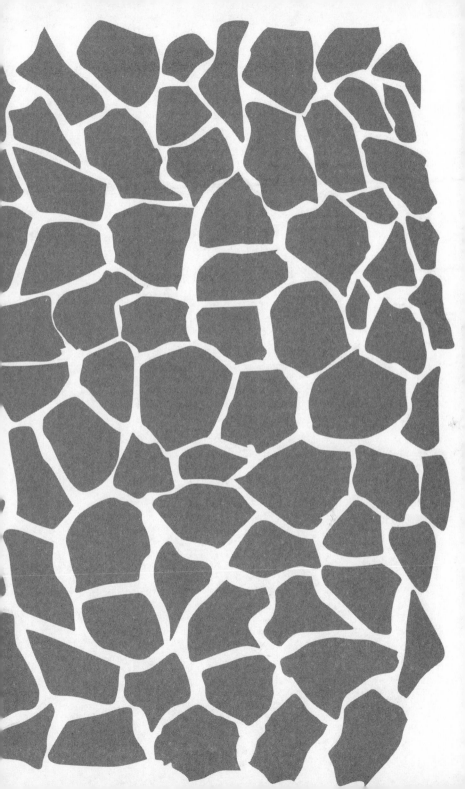

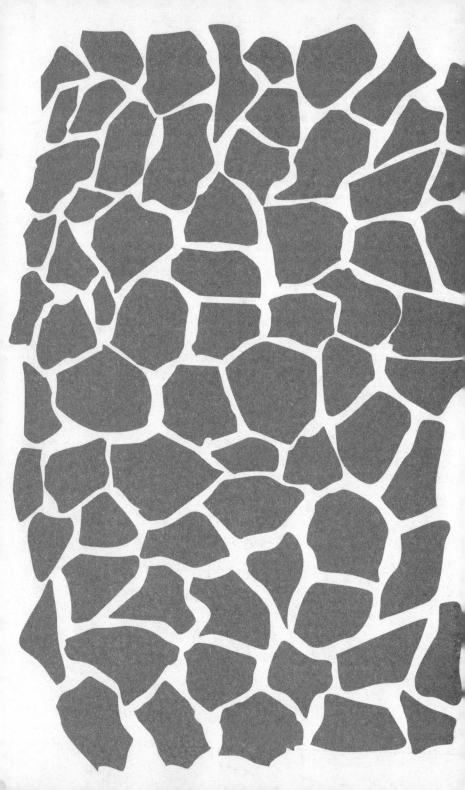